To Henry
The star of the story!
From Selina x

It's Christmas Eve and Henry and his family are at the North Pole to see the reindeer.

Henry is a little bit grumpy, he wanted to see Santa Claus as well, but Santa is FAR too busy preparing to deliver all the presents.

rumpy Henry kicks a clump of snow over one of the reindeer.

"Oh Henry, that's naughty, Santa Claus only visits good children, not naughty ones. You won't be on his good list!" Henry is reprimanded.

Henry kicks another clump of snow at the reindeer.

Whoops!

This time he slips and starts sliding down a snowy slope! He zips in and out of trees, faster and faster, round and down he zooms.

6

Suddenly, the slope transforms into a big red slide. Henry whizzes round and round. It's so much fun, but where is he going to end up?

He zips right off the end of the slide and lands perfectly into a bright red and green Elf suit.

Henry's eyes shine with delight. He's in Santa's Grotto!

Welcome to the Grotto

8

But something is wrong.
Wrapping paper, ribbons, bows,
name tags, and sticky tape are
flying all over the place.

"This is TERRIBLE,
a DISASTER, AWFUL,
not good at all!"
wails a bright-
red-haired Elf whose
name is Rusty.

"Whatever is the matter?" asks Henry.

Rusty peers at the oddly tall Elf and exclaims "The GOOD list is MISSING, VANISHED, DISAPPEARED! Without it, the good girls and boys won't get their presents!"

"Oh dear, that just won't do." says Henry. "Please let me help you, I'm great at finding things."

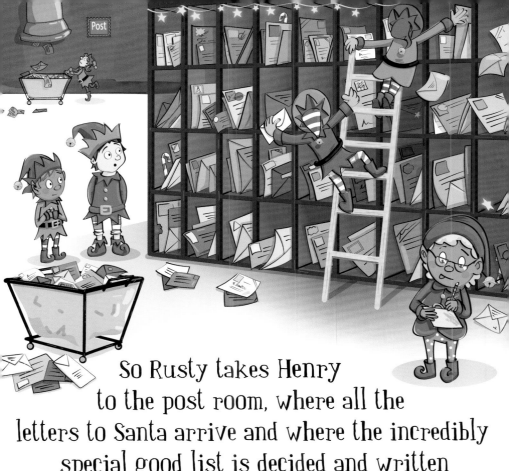

So Rusty takes Henry
to the post room, where all the
letters to Santa arrive and where the incredibly
special good list is decided and written
down very carefully in glittery ink.

Henry and Rusty look in the recycling containers...

...they search in the ribbon cupboard and explore under the gift boxes.

Henry even checks inside the oven, but the good list isn't there.

Henry asks the
other Elves if they have
seen the list, but they all
shake their heads.

13

When Henry and Rusty head outside to check with the snowman, Henry hears loud chewing and chomping coming from the stable where the reindeer live.

They see Comet and Cupid chewing on both ends of a long piece of paper. It looks suspiciously like a list!

"Oh NO, this is TERRIBLE!" cries Rusty.

Henry rushes to grab it and as he reads, he is extremely relieved to see what is written on it.

15

2 Dozen apples

10 sacks of carrots

4 Bags of flour

1 Jar of strawberry jam

3 Bags chestnuts

5 Onion

6 Sacks

8 Loaves of

Phew! It's actually Mrs Claus' shopping list and NOT the precious GOOD list, but time is running out, Santa Claus will soon be setting off to deliver the Christmas presents.

If the reindeer were munching on the shopping list, perhaps Mrs Claus has taken the good list by mistake?

They can't find Mrs Claus in the Grotto though as she's left to go grocery shopping...

...and Santa is already clambering into the big red sleigh to check the GOOD list twice!

17

Henry and Rusty jump into a
snowmobile. Would they find Mrs
Claus in time? If Santa doesn't leave
exactly at the right time, he won't
be able to deliver all the presents
before Christmas Day!

At the store they skid to a halt in front of a very startled Mrs Claus and quickly explain the problem.

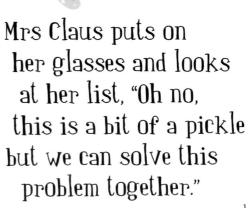

Mrs Claus puts on her glasses and looks at her list, "Oh no, this is a bit of a pickle but we can solve this problem together."

Mrs Claus calls Santa who booms "HO! HO! HO!" so loudly that it shakes the snow from the branches of the trees.

Santa zooms down in his sleigh to collect the priceless GOOD list and Rusty explains how GOOD Henry has been to help unravel the Christmas chaos.

"Thank you very much Henry, it's always important to be good and helpful and never naughty. You will definitely be on my GOOD list this year," says a very relieved and very thankful Santa Claus.

The end

COLOUR
ME IN